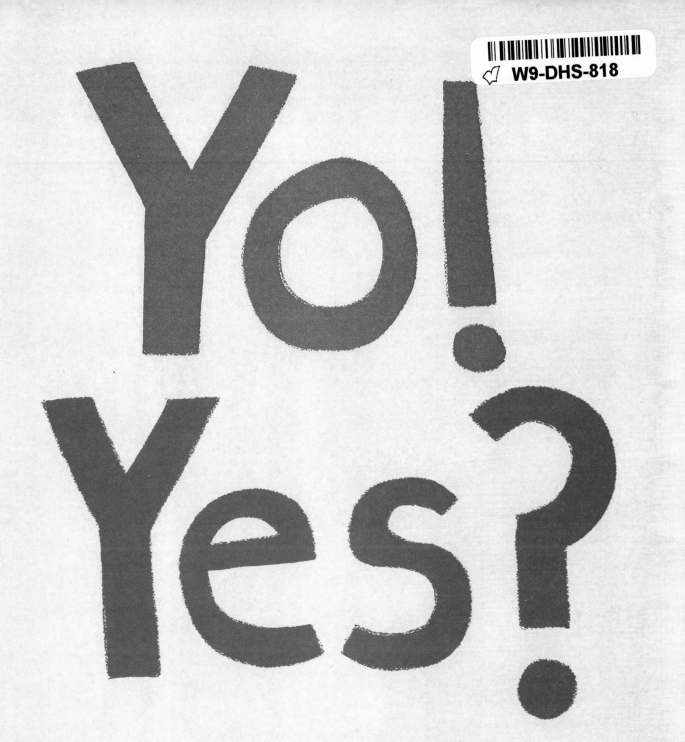

Yo! Yes?

BY

Chris Raschka

SCHOLASTIC INC.

NEW YORK   TORONTO   LONDON   AUCKLAND   SYDNEY

ISBN 0-590-20557-9

Copyright © 1993 by Christopher Raschka.
All rights reserved.
Published by Scholastic Inc., 555 Broadway, New York, NY 10012, by
arrangement with Orchard Books.

12 11 10 9 8 7 6 5 4 3 2 1   4 5 6 7 8 9/9

Printed in the U.S.A.   14

First Scholastic printing, September 1994

FOR

my parents

Yes ?

Hey!

Who?

You!

Me?

Yes,
you.

Oh.

What's up?

Not much.

Why?

No
fun.

Oh?

No
friends.

Yes.

Look!

Hmmm?

Me!

You?

Yes, me,!

You!

Well?

Well.

Yo!